THE KISS

A GAME OF ORAL SEX

VICTORIA RUSH

VOLUME 47

JADE'S EROTIC ADVENTURES - BOOK 47

COPYRIGHT

The Kiss © 2022 Victoria Rush

Cover Design © 2022 PhotoMaras

All Rights Reserved

For the uninhibited...

WANT TO AMP UP YOUR SEX LIFE?

Sign up for my newsletter to receive more free books and other steamy stuff. Discover a hundred different ways to wet your whistle!

Victoria Rush Erotica

1

When I received a new invitation to a party at my friend Madison's house, I couldn't wait to open the message. She always hosted the most interesting and sexy events, and with the cryptic subject heading *Kissing Game*, I could already feel my heart pounding as I began to read the message.

Dear Jade,

You are cordially invited to a party at my place this Saturday evening, starting at 9 p.m.

As with my previous events, there will be an exciting game designed to loosen everyone's inhibitions and get our juices flowing.

I don't want to give too much away, except to say you're likely to pick up some new pointers for spicing up your love life.

So get ready to mix it up with friends and foes alike, because in this game, there's no telling who or how you'll be paired up.

Be there or be square,

Maddy

P.S.: Make sure you're scrubbed clean, and I do mean every-where, because no area of your body will be off limits!

Holy cow, I thought after reading her message. *What in God's name has she dreamed up this time? No area off limits? Mixing it up with friends and foes?* I had no idea what she was planning, but she was right about one thing. It was definitely going to get my juices flowing.

As my mind began to wander about the hijinks she had in store, my hand slipped under my panties, imagining who might soon be kissing me all over my naked body...

When I arrived at Madison's house on the night of the party, she escorted me to her living room, where a group of people sat cross-legged around a large mattress covered with satin sheets. I recognized some of the faces in the crowd, but there were also quite a few new people I hadn't met before. With an even sprinkling of men and women, I scanned the crowd as everybody made small talk introducing themselves.

In addition to my friends Lily, Bonnie, and Emma, there was the sexy neighbor couple from the last party, Brad and Laura, plus my old friends from work, Ryan and Marco. But there were two new faces in the crowd that attracted most of my attention. One was a gorgeous African-American stud who looked like a young Denzel Washington, and the other was a stunning Asian girl who reminded me of the kick-ass actress, Lucy Liu. Rounding out the group was my trans-gender friend Shae and the full-figured Christina Hendricks lookalike from my tribbing workshop, Paige.

This should be interesting, I thought, squirming excitedly on the floor as I surveyed the beautiful assembly of men and women.

When the last guest arrived and was seated in the circle, Madison placed large wine goblets beside each of us, then she sat near the foot of the bed, passing two bottles of wine in each direction. After everyone had filled their glass, she pulled a packet of playing cards from her pocket and smiled at the group.

"First, I'd like to thank everyone for coming to my party," she said. "I know I was a little coy in my invitation about what I had planned, but those of you who've been to my previous parties know that's half the fun. Not knowing who you'll be paired with or what you'll be asked to do makes it all the more interesting."

Then she raised her glass, nodding to each of the participants.

"So, before we get started, I'd like to make a toast: to new friends and new discoveries!"

"Cheers to that," Emma said.

"Amen," the handsome African-American newcomer, Linc, said.

"Okay then," Maddy said after everybody took a large gulp of wine to loosen up. "You're probably wondering what kind of kissing game I've cooked up and how we can make such a seemingly innocent act a little more interesting."

She opened the packet of cards then placed the deck face-down between her legs.

"As always," she smiled. "Most of the fun is in the expectation and the surprise. But instead of using a spinning wheel this time to determine the match-ups, we're going to use a deck of cards."

She began pulling cards off the top of the deck and spinning them toward each person around the circle, and as they reached out to catch their card, they peering at it with a puzzled expression.

"Here's how it's going to work," Maddy smiled after everyone received a card. "The person with the highest card will be the one giving the kiss in each round, and the one with the lowest card will be the one receiving the kiss."

There was a brief moment of silence in the group, then Ryan raised his hand cautiously.

"Are we going to be kissing each other in the usual manner?" he said. "I mean, insofar as being restricted to kissing on the *lips*?"

"Well, that's where it gets interesting," Madison grinned. "The person with the high card will also get to choose where on the other person's body he or she wishes to kiss. And as I suggested in my party invitation, there is no area off limits. Subject to the agreement of your partner, of course. As always, this is a full consent zone."

"Are we going to be doing this fully *clothed*?" the full-figured redhead, Paige, said, winking in my direction.

"That's up to the two of you," Maddy nodded. "Depending on the area targeted, you might find the experience more titillating, in a matter of speaking, if you choose to expose a little skin."

"And this so-called *kiss*," Brad said, peering at his wife, Laura, to clarify the limits of the game. "Are we limited to lips-only contact, or are we allowed to engage certain *other* oral body parts to heighten the experience?"

Madison paused for a moment, smiling at Laura.

"If that's how you and your wife kiss, closed-mouthed like in those old black-and-white movies, then knock yourself out. But if you want to make it more interesting and exciting, then I encourage you to take a page out of the

French playbook and bring a little tongue action into the equation."

Everyone chuckled at the subtle dig at Brad's kissing technique, then the pretty Asian girl, Mei, raised her hand.

"Exactly how far are we allowed to go with these kisses?" she asked. "What if we start to get, you know, *aroused* by the experience? How will we know when to stop?"

"Something tells me you'll know when the time comes," Maddy smiled. "Like I said in my message, there are no limits with this game. I encourage each of you to explore the full range of possibilities until you're fully satisfied."

"So, there'll be no hourglass or egg-timer this time?" Marco chuckled.

"I'm not going to stop you just when things begin to get interesting," Madison nodded.

"What if we're handed an ace?" Shae said, turning her card around to reveal an ace of hearts. "Does that count as a low card or a high card?"

"I'll leave that up to the holder of the card," Madison smiled. "In that case, you can decide if you want to give or receive your kiss with the next lowest card holder."

"Mmm," Shae hummed, peering around the circle at the flushed faces of the already excited participants. "I'm starting to like this game already."

2

―――――

"Let's get started by everyone revealing their cards," Madison said.

Everybody flipped their cards around, with both Bonnie and Shae showing an ace and Emma showing a two.

"What do we do if we have the same card?" Shae said, frowning as she peered at Bonnie's high card.

"Well, since this is a game all about *kissing*," Maddy smiled. "We'll give hearts the highest rank, then diamonds, then spades, then clubs. Since you've got the highest card, Shae, you can decide if you wish to give or receive this turn."

Shae peered around the circle to see who had the next lowest card and when she saw it was the cute blonde, Emma, she grinned.

"I think I'll elect to be the one giving this time," she said.

"And which body part would you like to kiss in this instance?"

"Are you sure I only get to kiss *one*?" Shae said, running her eyes over Emma's slender but curvy figure.

"Those are the rules," Maddy nodded. "We've got to save

some of the other parts for the future rounds if we want to keep it interesting."

"In that case," Shae said, smiling toward Emma. "I think I'll choose her lips."

"Which ones?" Emma said, lifting an eyebrow.

"It's tempting," Shae said, glancing between her crossed legs. "But I want to start by kissing that pretty face of yours."

"Okay," Madison said, nodding toward the two girls. "Why don't the two of you make yourselves comfortable on the mattress so the rest of us can enjoy the show?"

Emma catwalked onto the middle of the bed, sitting upright with her arms extended behind her, then Shae slunk up next to her, resting beside her hips.

Shae peered at her partner for a moment, then she turned her head, kissing Emma gently on the side of her neck under her ear. Emma moaned softly, and I glanced expectantly toward Madison. Normally, she enforced the rules like an overprotective den mother, but this time she simply smiled at the two women, nodding for them to continue.

Shae continued kissing Emma's neck downward with soft kisses, and Emma lifted her chin, exposing her throat while Shae nibbled on it like a lion cub play-fighting with her sibling. With everyone looking on in rapt attention, I wondered how many of the guys were making mental notes about how to warm up their lovers with the tender display of foreplay. I wasn't sure how many of them even knew that Shae was transgender. Being a true hermaphrodite, she had fully functional male and female sex organs, but her hourglass figure and delicate facial features made her look one hundred percent like a feminine sex goddess.

"Are you getting as turned on as I am watching this?" Lily whispered, sitting next to me.

"Fuck yes," I panted. "I've been on the receiving end of those kisses, and I can tell you firsthand that Shae knows how to use every weapon in her arsenal to drive a woman crazy."

"It's too bad the roles weren't reversed," Lily nodded, squirming restlessly on the floor. "Cause I'd love to see some of those *other* body parts in action too."

"Something tells me this won't be the last we'll see of her this evening," I smiled.

As Shae began to slowly kiss her way up the underside of Emma's chin, she shifted into a kneeling position, raising one leg and straddling Emma's hips. The closer she moved toward her mouth, the wider Emma parted her lips, eagerly anticipating Shae's touch.

But just as she reached the bottom of her lower lip, Shae pulled away a few inches, just enough for them to feel their hot breath on each other's skin. While Shae tilted her face from side to side, she brushed her lips softly against Emma's opening, intimating about she intended to do next.

"She's giving a master class in kissing," Lily sighed. "I only wish the *guys* I dated knew how to do this half as well."

"Perhaps you should bring a few of them along next time," I chuckled. "The more we can educate, the better."

After teasing Emma with soft butterfly kisses for the better part of three minutes, Shae opened her mouth, clutching Emma's upper lip and sliding her tongue softly under the rim while feeling the ridges of her teeth. Emma tilted her head higher up, encouraging her to press deeper inside, but Shae seemed determined to go slow and explore every crevasse of the girl's soft and pliant cavity.

While Emma began to move her hips sensuously on the heaving mattress, Shae pulled one of her knees down, forcing Emma's legs apart as she slid her thigh up toward the crotch of Emma's tight jeans. When she pressed her leg against her cleft, Emma moaned into Shae's mouth and Shae raised her right hand, running her fingers softly through Emma's hair as she continued nibbling and sucking on her upper lip.

"Holy fuck," Lily panted next to me. "What I'd give to have that girl kissing my *pussy* like that right now."

"If you play your cards right," I smiled. "You might just have a chance later this evening."

As Emma began to rock her hips against Shae's pressing thigh, Shae lowered her head to suck on Emma's lower lip. While everybody looked on in mesmerized silence, I noticed a few of the men adjusting their package, obviously turned on by the erotic sight of the two women kissing so lustfully.

By now, Emma's mouth was wide open as Shae sucked, nibbled, and probed her with her tongue. When she pulled Shae closer toward her, pressing their tits together, Shae adjusted her leg to the outside of Emma's hips, sitting down over top of her crotch as they ground their pubises together. Shae lifted her other hand to the opposite side of Emma's head and pulled her face harder toward her, thrusting her tongue deep into her opening while they mashed their lips tightly together.

As the two women began kissing each other passionately and moaning into each other's mouths, Shae traced a line around the side of Emma's face with the tips of her fingers, starting above her eyebrows, then down over her soft cheekbones and along the crease of her jaw. When her hand reached the underside of her chin, Shae placed her fingers around the front of her neck, squeezing her throat as she began to kiss her more forcefully.

After a few minutes, Emma pulled away, gasping for air

as she peered into Shae's eyes with flared eyes. I wasn't sure if it was because Shae had been partially cutting off her air supply or Emma just wanted to show her partner what effect she was having on her. Either way, she wasn't the *only* one approaching the peak of her excitement while I noticed many of the other participants moving their hands between their legs as they watched the action unfolding on the mattress.

"Have you guys had *enough* yet?" Madison interjected, trying to tamp down the escalating tension in the room.

"Fuck no," Emma said, grabbing Shae's head with both of her hands and pulling her hard toward her. "We're just getting started."

As the two lovers continued twirling their tongues inside one another's mouths, they started to rock their hips together rhythmically. I noticed a bulge in Shae's pants and wondered if her hardening tool was providing some direct friction on Emma's clit under her tight jeans. But the reaction of the two women soon answered my question. As they began moaning more loudly and grinding their hips harder together, it was soon apparent that they were moving ever closer toward a mutual climax.

"Fuck *this*," Lily said, unbuttoning her jeans and thrusting three fingers under her soaking panties. "I can't wait any longer for my turn. I need a piece of this action right now."

"No kidding," I nodded, joining her in stimulating myself while we watched the sexy pair on the mattress.

By now, Emma and Shae were rocking their hips vigorously together, and I wondered why they hadn't removed their clothes, since Madison had given her approval to do so at the beginning. Whether it was because they knew they were only supposed to be touching their lips together or because they were already too far gone to interrupt their hot lovemaking session, I wasn't sure. But one thing was for certain – it wouldn't be long before the two of them reached the height of their passion.

As their moaning notched up in volume and frequency, they wrapped their arms around one another's backs, pulling their bodies harder together, then they began shaking in each other's arms, groaning and panting while they bit each other's lips tightly. It must have taken almost a full minute for each of them to come down from their powerful climaxes and when they finally finished shaking and convulsing, Shae pulled away to gently kiss the sides of Emma's swollen lips while she ran her fingers through her hair softly.

"Now *that's* what I call a kiss," Lily said, still playing with her pussy with her hands down her pants.

"Yes," I panted alongside her. "Who needs to be naked when you have a lover like *that* giving you all of her oral attention?"

When the two women finally separated and stood up to return to their previous places in the circle, I noticed the crotch of Emma's jeans had a wide stain in the front. But it was the front of *Shae's* pants that attracted most of the attention around the circle. Her enormous engorged cock was pointing forty-five degrees up toward the side of her hip, bulging prominently under the tight confines of her equally wet jeans.

"Holy shit," I grunted. "If that's how hot it gets from kissing only *lips to lips*, I can't wait to see what happens when we get to kiss some of the other interesting body parts."

3

———————

When the girls returned to their places in the circle, Madison smiled as she watched the men adjusting themselves in an obvious state of arousal.

"I hope you all enjoyed that little demonstration of oral love," she said. "I don't know about you guys, but *I* certainly picked up a few pointers for elevating my game."

"Definitely," Lily panted, zipping up the front of her jeans.

"Well, we're just getting started," Maddy nodded. "There's still a lot of other body parts to explore. Are you guys ready for the next round?"

Everybody nodded and returned their cards to Madison, then she shuffled the deck, tossing a new one to each participant. When they revealed their numbers, this time Laura held the high card and Paige had the lowest one.

"It looks like Laura will be the one giving this time, and Paige will be the one receiving," Madison said. "Have you decided which body part you'd like to kiss, Laura?"

Laura turned her head to examine Paige's full-figured

body wrapped up in a tight t-shirt and jeans, then her eyes bulged, staring at her huge melons.

"Um, I think I'd like to kiss Paige's *breasts*," she hesitated. "That is, if she doesn't mind my being so forward."

Paige placed her hands under her tits and playfully pushed them together, smiling back at Laura.

"Of course not," she purred. "I've been dying to unshackle these things all day. It'll be my pleasure."

"Mine too," Laura said, turning to wink at her husband before she shuffled over to the middle of the mattress.

As Paige crawled toward her on her hands and knees, everyone in the room stared at her magnificent round ass, looking more like it belonged on the back of a thoroughbred *mare* than the sexy redhead. When she sat down next to Laura, her partner paused for a moment to inspect her Rubenesque figure, then she pressed Paige's back down onto the mattress. She climbed on top of her, straddling her hips with bent knees, then she leaned forward, slowly sliding her palms up her torso. When she reached Paige's big globes, she curled her fingers around the edges, massaging and teasing her while the redhead panted below her.

"Mmm," Laura grunted, peering over in the direction of her husband, who was looking on in a catatonic trance. "I bet you wish I was built like *this* goddess, don't you?"

"You're perfect just the way you are," Brad lied. "But I'm enjoying your worshipping her from this position at the foot of the altar."

Laura leaned forward to whisper something in Paige's ear and they both chuckled. Then she began kissing her way down Paige's upper body until she reached the top of her mounds, pausing to bury her face in Paige's deep cleavage. I watched her back heaving as she breathed in the perfume of Paige's decolletage, and for a moment, I was transported back to our last encounter at Laila's tribbing workshop, where I got to play with them firsthand.

After a few seconds, she lifted her head, nibbling toward the tips of Paige's mountains, stopping at the top to bite each of her thick nipples until her t-shirt was soaked with two dark rings of saliva. Laura sat up for a moment to admire her handiwork, then she shook her head in disbelief.

"Jesus, girl," she panted. "Those have to be the most magnificent tits I've ever seen on a woman. Can you share your secret for building a bosom like that?"

"I suspect it's mostly genetics," Paige chuckled. "But if you're not afraid to put on a few extra pounds, some of that additional weight will migrate to your bustline eventually."

Laura turned back to glance at her husband and grinned.

"What do you say, dear?" she said. "Would you like me to gain a few extra bra sizes if it means I'll be plumper every-where *else*?"

"All the more to love," Brad smiled.

"Well, I don't know about the rest of you guys," Laura said, peering at the other participants around the circle. "But I'm dying to see what these girls look like untethered."

She turned her head to glance at Paige, and smiled.

"May I?"

"By all means," Paige nodded. "I've been waiting all this time to feel those lips on my skin."

Laura reached behind Paige's shoulders and pulled her up into a sitting position, then she pulled her t-shirt over her shoulders and reached behind her back to unclasp her bra. As she pulled the straps around to the front and let the brassiere fall to the side of the mattress, everyone around the circle gasped. Paige's giant breasts looked almost as big as a cow's udder, with thick, protruding nipples to match.

"Oh my God," Laura panted, gawking at them like a twelve-year-old seeing his first centerfold. "They're exquisite. And *firm*. And natural..."

"Of course," Paige said, kissing Laura on her flushed cheeks. "Are you just going to *stare* at them or were you thinking of touching them? This is a *kissing* game, after all."

Laura peered into her hazel eyes for a moment then she lowered her head, unable to resist the siren call of Paige's protruding bullets. She drew them hard into her mouth like a suckling pig, and Paige moaned, arching her back to press her mounds harder against Laura's face.

"Damn," Lily said next to me, watching the pair with dilated pupils. "That is one magnificent set of tits. You know I lean more toward *men*, but you wouldn't have to twist my arm to persuade me to rub myself against that voluptuous body if I had the chance."

"Well, it's still a card game," I smiled. "You've got as good a chance as any."

While Laura sucked and nibbled on each of Paige's hard teats in turn, she squeezed her small hands around her huge orbs like a schoolgirl caressing a Greek statue. I peered around the group, noticing everyone's mouths parted slack-jawed as they squirmed on the floor beside the mattress, wishing it was their turn to worship the gorgeous redhead instead of Laura.

After a few minutes, Laura grew tired of bending down to lick Paige's breasts, and she pressed her back down onto the mattress, straddling her waist between her thighs. She took a minute to appraise the shape of Paige's breasts resting with the full force of gravity weighing down on them, then she shook her head, marveling at how tall and upright they were, even when she was lying down.

"I wouldn't have believed these were real if I hadn't felt

them with my own *hands*," she said, staring at Paige's bosom like she was admiring a masterpiece in an art gallery.

"Not to mention your *lips*," Paige smiled, pulling Laura back down toward her. "Don't forget your lips."

Laura lowered her head toward Paige's chest and her long hair brushed over her mounds, then she paused halfway to tilt her head from side to side, caressing Paige's dark medallions with the tips of her strands.

"Mmm," Paige purred. "That feels heavenly. Caress my nipples with your silky hair."

"That's not the *only* body part I'd like to caress them with," Laura smiled, glancing in Madison's direction to make sure she wasn't going too far astray.

Maddy peered back at her for a moment, shaking her head slowly.

"We've already given you plenty of extra license using your hands and other parts to caress her," she said. "But as long as you stay fully clothed, I'll give you a little more room to maneuver."

"Well, in *that* case," Laura said, leaning down to press her breasts covered in a silk blouse against Paige's bare tits.

"Yes," Paige groaned, rolling her body on the mattress to feel Laura's tits rubbing against hers. "I can feel your hard nipples tweaking mine. I only wish I could return the favor–"

"The night is still young," Laura grinned, leaning down to kiss Paige passionately on the mouth.

"*Ahem,*" Madison said, clearing her throat. "As much as I'm sure you two would like to engage certain other body parts, this is supposed to be about kissing Paige's *tits*. There's still plenty of skin to titillate and excite lower down."

"Indeed there is," Laura said, raising up and scanning Paige's heaving chest. "But are you sure we've got enough time to give those beautiful mounds proper attention? Because I could spend all *day* kissing and lapping up those lambchops."

"How about five more minutes?" Madison said, noticing some of the other group members touching themselves impatiently. "We've still got a few more rounds to go through, and from the look of things, I think a few of the other participants are eager to have their turn in the spotlight."

"We better make the most of it then," Laura said, shifting her hips further down over Paige's pelvis and spreading her knees wider apart. "You said as long as we keep our clothes on, anything's fair game, right?"

"Within reason, yes," Madison nodded.

As Laura lowered her head back down toward Paige's bulging teats, she began to grind her pussy over the front of her jeans, creating a widening wet spot along her seam.

"Yes," Paige panted, rolling her hips in tandem with Laura. "Rub your pussy against my clit. If you keep licking my nipples like that, I'm going to come soon."

"Mmm," Laura grunted, twirling her tongue around Paige's thumb-sized berries like she was licking a lollypop. "I haven't had this much fun fully clothed since I first laid eyes on my husband."

Brad peered at his wife, grinding her pussy against Paige, then he reached into his pants to straighten out his straining cock.

"Um, I'm pretty sure we never had quite that much fun with our clothes on," he chuckled.

"You don't mind, baby?" Laura said, keeping her eyes focused on Paige's hardening tips.

"Are you kidding?" he said, rolling his fingers over his

dripping crown. "You're not the *only* one who's enjoying this show right now."

I smiled as I watched the rest of the group caressing their nipples and stroking their crotches while they gazed at the duo grinding and rocking their bodies together on the bouncing mattress.

"It looks like Maddy's allowing a little more stretching of the rules than usual," I said, elbowing Lily.

"Yeah," she panted, twirling her fingers under the front of her jeans as she stared at the sexy couple in front of us. "Thank God, because those two aren't the *only* ones who need to get off right now."

As Laura and Paige began to grind their hips harder together, Laura started to squeeze Paige's tits tighter between her hands, licking her nipples like a hungry baby. It didn't take long for the two of them to begin groaning louder as they neared the peak of their excitement.

"Yes, baby," Paige panted, tilting her head up to watch Laura sucking her teats. "Suck my nipples harder. I'm going to come soon."

Laura pressed her face harder down onto Paige's tits, then Paige grasped the back of her head while she arched her back in mounting ecstasy.

"God, yes," she hissed. "Yes, yes, yes – *guhhh!*"

As Paige started to convulse in pleasure under Laura's rocking hips, Laura angled her hips forward, pressing her cunt harder against Paige's wet crotch. I saw the wet spot in her pants darken as she squirted into her jeans, holding onto Paige's teat for dear life.

"Mhhh," Lily moaned beside me, starting to shake along with the others around the circle who also had their hands down their pants.

Up to this point I'd been so focused on soaking up

Paige's magnificent figure that I'd completely ignored my own mounting arousal. But I was so worked up that it only took a few seconds of touching my dripping pussy to come along with everyone else.

"Jesus," I panted after recovering from my brief but intense orgasm. "This is almost as much fun *watching* as participating in the action. It looks like Maddy's hit another home run. Pretty soon, her parties are going to become so popular, they'll be first come, first served only."

"Yeah," Lily sighed, leaning back against her outstretched arms to recover from her own powerful climax. "And there's no telling who'll be the first to come."

4

———

"Wow," Madison exhaled deeply, when Paige and Laura returned to their places in the circle. "Who knew kissing could be so much fun?"

"It helps when you have a canvas like *that* to work with," Laura said, smiling toward Paige.

"And when you have a master like Laura applying the brush strokes," Paige grinned.

"Something tells me there'll be plenty more masterpieces yet to come," Maddy nodded, noticing the bulges in the pants of many of the men sitting around the circle. "Shall we get started with another round?"

"Yes please," Brad grunted.

After Madison collected the cards and reshuffled the deck, she passed everyone a new card. This time the new girl, Mei, got the high number and Brad held the lowest.

"It looks like we're going to mix it up a little this time," Maddy smiled. "Mei holds the high card and Brad has the lowest, so it's Mei's turn to choose which body part she wishes to kiss."

Mei peered toward Brad, noticing his large erection straining against his tight jeans, then she smiled at Laura.

"I think it's only fair since his wife enjoyed a little extra-curricular activity in the last round that he gets an equal degree of attention. I'm hungry for some cock about now – that is, if Brad's feeling up to it."

"Oh, I'm feeling *up* for it alright," he smiled, turning to peer at Laura. "That is, if my wife doesn't mind my freeing my python."

"Knock yourself out, dear," Laura chuckled. "Maybe I'll pick up a few techniques to keep things interesting in the bedroom."

As the two players crawled toward the center of the mattress, I noticed Laura's eyes darting over Mei's sexy figure with a tinge of jealousy, and I wondered if it was such a good idea that they'd come to the party together. When Brad and Mei sat down beside one another, Mei slid her hand between his legs, caressing his throbbing member overtop of his moist jeans, then she glanced over at Madison.

"You said at the beginning that we could expose a little *skin* when we do this," she said. "Am I allowed to take off his clothes?"

"In the target area, yes," Maddy nodded. "So long as you keep the rest of your bodies covered. Mouth to penis only, those are the rules."

"Okay then," Mei said, peering at Brad's straining crotch. "Let's get you out of those tight pants. I think that snake of yours needs a little room to breathe."

As Mei slowly unbuckled his belt, I noticed Laura's face growing tenser, and I wasn't sure if it was because she was becoming envious of the other woman's attention, or because she was trying to suppress her own arousal at the thought of watching her husband having sex with the pretty Asian.

When Mei unzipped Brad's fly, he raised his hips then she pulled his trousers down over his ankles. When his dick flopped up and slapped against his belly, many of the women around the circle bulged their eyes, admiring his impressive package. Standing eight inches in height and at least six inches in circumference, his circumcised rod stood tall and proud, already glistening with a layer of precum oozing over his crown.

"Mmm," Mei said, kneeling between his legs and sliding her index finger up the underside of his pole from the base of his balls to his tip. "That looks delicious."

When she reached the sensitive skin on the underside of his glans, his dick twitched, emitting a drop of precum over the top of his flaring helmet.

"And I see you've already added some marinade to make my meal even more appetizing."

She leaned down, lifting her sexy ass in the air, and extended her long tongue, swiping it slowly up the length of his cock as she'd done with her finger. But this time, when she reached the head, his cock flapped excitedly, bouncing against his hard abs like a flagpole in a heavy wind.

I noticed that the position of the pair on the mattress had placed the angle of Brad's legs directly facing Laura, and as Mei continued to tease his cock with her tongue, Laura angled her body, trying to get a closer look at what Mei was doing. I smiled, realizing it probably wasn't an accident the way Mei had positioned herself, trying to block her view.

"Let the games *begin*," I nudged Lily beside me. "I'm not sure Laura's going to enjoy this quite as much as her husband."

"What's good for the goose is good for the gander," Lily chuckled, staring at Brad's impressive pecker.

As he arched his back to give Mei freer access to his pulsing tool, Mei tilted her head while she drew circles over his darkening crown, slopping up his rivers of precum with the flat side of her tongue. When she began flicking it against his sensitive frenulum, he tilted his head back, moaning in pleasure.

"Looks like this isn't her first rodeo," I nodded to Lily.

"Mmm," she hummed approvingly. "Something tells me she's had a little practice doing this before."

"Are you taking notes?"

"Yes, while my quiver is still wet."

After a few minutes of teasing Brad with the tip of her tongue, Mei pushed Brad down onto the mattress and raised his knees, spreading his legs apart. Then she lay down on her stomach with her head in front of his crotch, lapping at his balls like a puppy dog. I noticed that Brad was freshly shaved in his perineum, and I wondered how much of his manscaping had been motivated by his anticipation of this evening's events as opposed to his usual marital routine. Either way, I noticed his wife looking on in rapt attention, now that she had a clear view of the show.

While Mei lapped and tugged on his scrotum with the tips of her teeth, he flexed his buttocks, raising his cock higher in the air as it flapped excitedly over the shaved stubble of his mound.

"That is one *fuckable* dick," Lily sighed, squirming on the floor next to me.

"You're not going to touch yourself this time?" I said.

"I don't want to miss one second of this performance," she nodded. "Besides, my fingers would be a poor substitute for that magnificent organ."

As Mei threaded her hands behind Brad's knees, the further she pushed his legs up toward his chest, the lower she began licking and nibbling toward his anus.

"Um, *hello*," Madison interrupted. "I hate to put a damper on your fun, but you're moving a little far astray from the target area."

"It's all part of the same erogenous zone," Mei protested, pausing her head.

"That may be true," Madison nodded. "But that *particular* erogenous zone you're moving toward has its own set of inducements. I'd like to save that one for its own dedicated attention later on, if someone so wishes."

"Fine," Mei huffed, pretending to be upset. "I guess I'll just have to focus on certain *other* areas. Am I still allowed to touch his balls?"

"I think those are connected close enough to the main attraction to count as part of the package," Madison smiled, peering toward Brad. "What do you say, Brad? Is it okay if Mei caresses your balls in addition to your penis?"

"If you *insist*," he chuckled.

Mei raised up on her knees and rested her ass on her feet, then she grabbed his dick with two hands and slid her mouth over his knob, engulfing his pole halfway down his length. As she gripped the base of his shaft with her fists, Brad pumped his organ in and out of her mouth, flexing his buttock muscles while he groaned loudly.

"*That's* what I'm talking about," Lily panted. "I'd let that stud cum in my mouth any time."

"I don't expect he'll be long for this world," I nodded, appreciating Mei's multi-pronged attack on his purple phallus.

As Brad began to hump Mei's face more vigorously, she lowered her hands and clasped his balls while his face began to flush more deeply. But just as he seemed ready to erupt, she suddenly pulled her face away from his organ, and it flapped wildly, inches away from her lips. At first, I thought she'd pulled away because she didn't want him coming in her mouth, but as she peered into Brad's eyes with a sly smile, she bobbed her head back down over his dick, tickling his perineum with the tips of her fingers while he grunted in delirious pleasure.

As his pleasure escalated toward its inevitable climax, Mei shifted one hand to the base of his erection while squeezing his balls tighter with her other hand. As he gradually lifted his hips off the surface of the mattress, she stepped up the pace of her bobbing head, twisting it from side to side to provide an extra degree of stimulation over his sensitive glans.

Suddenly, he reached out to grasp the back of Mei's head, and he howled like a wolf as his knees buckled and his buttocks quivered in the midst of an orgasm that seemed to last forever. The whole time he was shaking, Mei kept her mouth over his pulsating organ, gulping to swallow down his enormous load. When he finally stopped shaking and moaning, he fell back onto the mattress and flopped his arms out to the side, breathing heavily.

I glanced over in the direction of his wife, noticing her hands were down the front of her pants, jilling herself rapidly as she shook in simultaneous pleasure.

"I guess Laura wasn't as jealous as I thought at the idea of another woman sucking her husband's cock," I said to Lily.

"Yes," Lily nodded. "I have a feeling this isn't the *first* time those two have enjoyed a little two-way swinging action."

5

———————

"Whew," Madison said, pretending to wipe her brow after Brad and Mei returned to the circle. "Is it getting warm in here or what? That was some pretty hot kissing."

"I think there was a lot more than just *kissing* going on there," Laura said, elbowing her husband hard in the ribs.

"Well, as long as the one administering it uses his or her *mouth*, as far as I'm concerned, anything's fair game."

Madison glanced at the satin sheets, noticing a large wet spot in the middle of the mattress.

"Why don't we all take a little bio break before we start the next round?" she said. "You might want to top up your liquid courage before we resume, because something tells me it's going to get even more titillating moving forward."

While everybody took a moment to freshen up and top up their wine glasses, Madison changed the sheets and collected the cards. I noticed Brad and Laura took a little longer than the others to return to the circle and when they did, their cheeks looked flushed.

"I guess Laura couldn't wait any longer for her turn at the other end," I smiled to Lily.

"That was some seriously hot foreplay in the last round," she nodded. "If *my* husband were here, I'd have taken him to a private room too."

While Madison reshuffled the deck, she peered around the group.

"I hope everyone had a chance to clean up and prepare for a new round," she said. "Because there's still quite a few unexplored places still to kiss, and I for one am looking forward to some interesting new combinations."

After everyone received their new card and turned them around, it was Ryan who held the highest card while the hot African-American newcomer, Linc, held the lowest.

"Oh goody," Lily smiled when she saw the outcome. "I've been waiting for some hot boy-on-boy action."

"This should be good," I nodded. "I know Ryan's hard-core gay, and from the looks of things, the new guy seems pretty straight."

"Okay," Madison said, looking at everyone's cards. "It looks like Ryan drew the high card and Linc has the lowest. Which body part would you like to kiss this time, Ryan?"

Ryan paused for a moment as he peered at Lincoln's broad shoulders and muscular thighs.

"You know I can never pass up an opportunity to worship another pretty cock," he smiled.

"What do you say, Linc?" Madison said, glancing at her new guest. "Are you up for a little man-to-man oral satisfaction?"

"Um–" Lincoln hesitated, peering around the circle as if he was embarrassed to hook up with another man.

"Oh, come on," Madison said. "You're among friends here. You know what they say, you should try everything at least once. You never know if you'll like it until you give it a try."

Lincoln tilted his head, then sighed deeply.

"I guess if I'm the one on the *receiving* end, it can't hurt," he said with a lopsided smile.

"Oh, I'm pretty sure it won't *hurt*," Ryan chuckled, sashaying over toward the center of the mattress with a Cheshire Cat grin on his face.

When Linc sat down cautiously beside him, Ryan caressed his shoulders, then slid his hands sexily down the side of his V-shaped torso.

"Are sure I can't take off the *rest* of his clothes?" Ryan said, peering toward Maddy with a wrinkled forehead. "Because I'm pretty sure I'm not the *only* one in this room who'd like to see this stud fully uncovered."

"I suspect you're right about that," Madison said, glancing around the circle at the drooling women admiring Lincoln's muscular physique. "But rules are rules. It'll have to be just his pants."

"Pants it is," Ryan grinned, peering into Lincoln's flushed face with a devious smile.

As he began unbuttoning the handsome African-American's fly, I noticed the front of his jeans bulging, and when Ryan pulled them down to his knees, his thick organ flopped out, pointing off to the side. Everybody could see the sinewy muscles and ligaments of his lightly shaved mound above his caramel-colored, semi-erect dick, and I was sure they were all thinking the same thing.

"Shit," Lily hissed next to me. "Why do the *gay* guys have all the fun?"

"Something tells me it's not just the gay guy who's going to enjoy this little episode," I said, noticing Linc's dark dick slowly lengthening and rising as Ryan cupped his balls and tickled the curly black hair over his pubis.

As he continued to tease Linc around the base of his penis with the tips of his fingers, Lincoln's organ continued to rise until it was standing straight up, extending two full inches above his navel.

"Oh my God," Lily gasped, staring at Linc's flapping totem. "How will he even get his lips around that thing?"

"I'm pretty sure Ryan's had his share of well-equipped lovers," I nodded. "Just watch and enjoy."

When Linc's cock had reached its fully engorged length, Ryan wrapped his two hands around his soda-can-thick shaft and pulled the skin down, exposing his huge, bulging crown under his foreskin. He took a moment to admire Lincoln's impressive package, then he lowered his head to suck on the glistening bulb like a boy with a lollypop. Linc closed his eyes and tilted his head back, trying to conceal his growing pleasure.

"I wonder what it feels like to get head from a man for the first time?" Lily said, squirming excitedly on the floor.

"I dunno," I smiled. "But from the looks of things, this isn't the first time he's fantasized about it."

"Well, they say everyone's at least a *little* bit bi," Lily nodded.

"I think *any* red-blooded dude would turn gay for a moment if they could get their hands on that magnificent piece of meat."

While Ryan rolled his tongue expertly around the rim of his partner's erection, Linc slowly raised his body up onto his knees, pressing his hips further forward toward Ryan's face. Recognizing the signal that he was enjoying his ministrations, Ryan slowly lowered his lips over Lincoln's pole until he engulfed it all the way down to the base.

"Holy *fuck*," Lily grunted. "How can he even do that? That thing must be halfway down his throat!"

"Most gay guys learn how to relax their throat muscles when they go down on their partners. It's really just a matter of learning how to control your gag reflex."

"I don't see how I wouldn't gag on that firehose. He'd fairly rip me apart with that giant dagger."

"I guess it's a good thing you weren't chosen as his partner then," I chuckled. "Because something tells me Ryan's about to put on a master's class for giving head."

When Ryan swallowed the whole length of Lincoln's dick, Linc placed his hands over the back of his head and looked down, thrusting his hips hard against Ryan's face. I smiled knowing Linc had probably never received a blow job like this before, and his eyes flared while he bucked Ryan's face like a wild animal. Ryan reached around his back to grab his powerful flexing buttocks, and Lincoln began grunting more loudly, getting ready to empty his load down Ryan's throat.

But just as he was about to erupt, Ryan lifted his head off Lincoln's cock and grinned up at him while Linc gazed back with a puzzled look. Ryan didn't say a word, then flipped over onto his back while he straightened his dick under his tight jeans as he peered up at Lincoln's tight balls and sweaty crack.

"I want you to fuck me *this* way," Ryan said, smiling up at the muscular Adonis.

"*Fuck* you?" Linc said, pinching his eyebrows together. "How do you mean?"

"The same way you were before, just from a different angle," Ryan said. "This way, you'll be fully in control."

Ryan tilted his head back, then opened his mouth as wide as he could, nodding for Lincoln to insert his dick in his mouth. Linc peered at his unusual position for a moment, then he spread his legs further apart and pointed his instrument into Ryan's willing mouth, slowly inserting it deeper and deeper while Ryan relaxed his throat. Within seconds, he'd inserted his entire length down Ryan's gullet as he began humping his face, watching his partner eagerly swallowing his manhood.

"Holy fuck!" Lily gasped next to me. "I've never seen anything like that before."

"Welcome to the world of gay sex," I chuckled, watching Ryan's hips dry-humping the air while Lincoln skull-fucked his head.

Linc leaned forward and placed the palms of his hands beside Ryan's hips, watching Ryan's erect dick bulging under his pants, then he looked up, peering in Madison's direction.

Madison paused for a moment as if reading his mind, then she nodded quietly. While Ryan continued rocking his hips, Linc unbuttoned his jeans to free his straining hard-on, and when it popped up, Lincoln lowered his head without hesitation to suck on his head voraciously. He couldn't take as much of Ryan's dick as was being reciprocated on the other end, but with Ryan's smaller penis, he was able to get at least half of it in his mouth.

"It seems like Lincoln likes dick more than he's let on," Lily smiled.

"Like you said," I nodded. "Everybody turns a little bit bi when the right opportunity presents itself."

As I glanced around the circle at the rest of the group, I noticed virtually every guy had their hands down their pants, rubbing their hard cocks while the women seemed just as turned on, circling their clits. Even *Madison* seemed aroused by the spectacle, rubbing her wet crotch as she watched the two men sixty-nining one another.

It didn't take long for them to approach the height of their pleasure while they pounded each other's faces, and as they began to hump each other harder and faster, their moaning grew progressively louder until they both grunted loudly, pressing their dicks hard against each other faces. When Lincoln came, his buttock muscles contracted tightly as he rammed his spear balls-deep against Ryan's chin while Ryan moaned in delirious pleasure, emptying his own burgeoning load into Lincoln's moaning mouth.

After they both finished climaxing, Lincoln pulled his dripping tool out of Ryan's mouth and zipped up his pants, nodding silently to his partner. When they both returned to their previous places in the circle, you could hear a pin drop in the room while everybody stared at the two of them with equally flushed faces, utterly awestruck at what they'd just witnessed.

6

———

"**L**ike I said," Madison interjected after a few seconds, breaking the awkward tension in the room. "Things were going to get a little more interesting the further we moved along. I don't know about the *rest* of you guys, but that was one of the hottest things I've ever seen. Kudos to both men for showing us how much fun two people can have when they let their guard down a few inches."

"I think it was more than just a *few* inches," Bonnie chuckled, still staring at Linc's bulging jeans.

"Who's ready to push it one step further?" Madison smiled.

Everyone raised their hands and she tossed them a new card, and this time Marco displayed the high number while Bonnie held the lowest.

"Mmm," Madison hummed. "We haven't had any boy-on-girl kissing yet. Looks like you're going to be the one in charge this time, Marco. What body part of Bonnie's would you like to kiss?"

Marco peered toward Bonnie and she smiled back at him, slowly spreading her legs apart.

"It seems we've missed one body part so far," he said, staring at the wet spot in her crotch. "If Bonnie's game, I'd love to give her pretty kitty some oral attention."

"What do you say, Bonnie?" Madison said, turning toward her sexy friend.

"I thought he'd *never* ask," Bonnie chuckled, running her eyes over Marco's slender, athletic physique.

When they joined together in the middle of the mattress, they sat upright on their knees facing one another, staring into each other's eyes. Marco leaned forward a few inches and angled his head, pretending to kiss her softly. While she closed her eyes awaiting his touch, the other women squirmed uncomfortably, wishing they were the ones on the opposite side of the handsome Latino's sensuous caresses.

"I hope you're not going to tease me like this when you go further down," Bonnie panted, opening her eyes to glare at Marco in mock outrage. "Because it's not going to work if you just stare at me and *breathe* on me the entire time."

"We'll have to see about that," Marco smiled, reaching down to unbutton her jeans.

As he lowered her zipper, she tilted her head upward, and Marco blew softly on her neck. While he tugged gently on her jeans, she rocked her hips from side-to-side, until they dropped down to the bottom of her knees. Marco placed one hand behind her back and slowly lowered her onto the mattress, then he gently pulled her pant legs down over her ankles, one at a time.

"This guy's obviously had some practice doing this before," Lily said, breathing heavily next to me.

"It looks like he's in no hurry to get down to business," I nodded, feeling my own panties dampening while I watched his sexy display of foreplay.

"Slow is good," Lily panted. "Especially with a Valentino like that doing the kissing."

After Marco pulled Bonnie's jeans down over her feet, he spread her ankles apart then kneeled between her legs, slowly sliding his palms up over the top of her trembling legs. When he reached the bottom of her panties, he threaded his thumbs under the lower seam, sliding them up along the crest of her hipbones, pausing when he reached the waistband. But instead of pulling them down over Bonnie's writhing hips, he leaned forward to kiss her stomach softly, nibbling on the waistband with his teeth as he pulled it teasingly away from her skin.

"Yes," Bonnie cooed, mesmerized by his expert technique. "Pull my panties off with your teeth. I want to feel your soft lips on my pussy."

But instead of pulling off her briefs, he slid the tip of his tongue under the waistband, sliding it toward the edges of her hips, dampening it with his warm saliva.

"Fuck yeah," Lily grunted, pressing her fingers under the front of her pants. "Those aren't the *only* panties he's making wet right now."

"I'm pretty sure *every* woman in this room is moist watching this guy work his magic," I nodded, squirming along with the rest of the girls while I watched the curly locks on the back of Marco's head while he teased Bonnie with his tongue.

As he pulled her panties ever-lower with his teeth, he swiped his thick stubble over the smooth surface of her shaved pubis while she raised and rocked her hips against his face, practically begging him to plant his mouth over her aching pussy. When he finally revealed the slit at the base of her mound, all the men in the room groaned, adjusting their hardening dicks as they watched Bonnie writhing on the mattress.

"I hope all those other guys are taking some cues from this Casanova," Lily groaned. "Because if they were even half as good at pleasing a woman as he is, they'd have a steady stream of them breaking down their doors in no time."

"Madison wasn't kidding when she said we were going to pick up a few pointers for spicing up our love life," I nodded. "I've already picked up a bunch of new moves I want to try out on my next lover."

After Marco pulled Bonnie's panties down below her knees, he gently raised each of her feet, pulling her panties off her legs, one leg at a time. Then he placed her undergarment on the mattress beside her feet and slowly raised her knees, shifting his body closer toward her junction. With Bonnie now exposing her dripping pussy inches from his face, he leaned down, kissing his way slowly up the inside of her thighs.

But instead of moving toward her apex, he kissed around the edges of her pussy, breathing in her sweet musk while gently pressing her legs further apart. By the time her knees were up around the sides of her chest, her flaring snatch was gaping wide open, dripping rivers of lubrication down over her perineum and under the crack of her ass.

"Jesus Christ," Lily panted next to me. "If he doesn't start sucking that pussy soon, I'm going to go over there and do it *for* him."

"All in due course, my dear," I smiled. "Most of the fun is in the journey, not in the destination."

"Tell that to poor Bonnie. She's likely to burst a gasket if he doesn't stem that hemorrhage pretty soon."

As if reading her mind, Marco tilted his body down and lowered his face to the base of Bonnie's slit, lapping up her juices with the flat side of his tongue like he was licking the side of a dripping ice cream cone. When his tongue passed over the top of her flaring bulb, she groaned, tilting her hips upward, begging him to suck her harder.

But he seemed determined to build up her tension before focusing on her glistening fruit, poised at the top of her folds like a ripe apple waiting to be plucked. While everyone rubbed their crotches staring at her flaring gash, Bonnie rolled and rocked her hips, begging Marco to take her into his mouth. By the time he finally pursed his lips and placed it over her burning gland, she'd already reached the peak of her excitement. When he began sucking her jewel and rolling his tongue over the nub with gentle figure-eight motions, she grabbed his ears, pulling him harder toward her dripping snatch.

"Fuck, yes," she groaned. "Suck my clit, Marco. I'm going to come so hard in your mouth. I haven't been kissed like this in such a long time."

Marco simply nodded softly while keeping a steady rhythm on her nub as she raised her hips higher and higher over the surface of the mattress. He placed his hands under her buttocks to help support her weight, and when she finally came, her hips buckled wildly while she screamed at the top of her lungs.

"Yes," she howled. "Suck me, baby. I'm coming in your beautiful mouth. Oh God, you know how to make love to a woman. *Ngahh!*"

While Bonnie came hard in Marco's mouth, I noticed all the other men and women around the circle groaning along with her as Lily flapped her knees against mine, jerking her body in simultaneous pleasure. By the time everyone finished groaning in mutual ecstasy, I was sure Madison's neighbors would be calling the cops by now, wondering just what kind of moral degeneracy was going on inside her darkened living room.

7

———

"Now *that's* how to make love to a lady," Madison smiled after Marco and Bonnie returned to their places. "Who else feels like adding Marco's number to the speed dial on their phones?"

When every woman's hand shot up, Madison chuckled while shuffling the cards in preparation for the next round.

"We still have a few guests that haven't participated yet," she said, peering over in Lily's and my direction. "Here's hoping we can get the *rest* of you as well stimulated before the evening is over."

She flipped the cards one at a time around the circle, and when everyone revealed their number, this time Emma held the high card and I held the lowest one.

"Mmm," Madison smiled. "I've been waiting for this match-up all night. Have you decided which of Jade's body parts you'd like to kiss this time, Emma?"

Emma peered over toward me, and I grinned, reading her mind. Ever since our all-girls' camping trip last summer, I'd been dying to have the pretty coed back in my arms and under my hips.

"As much as I'd love to kiss every inch of her sexy body," Emma said, running her eyes over my figure. "There's one spot that I've been fantasizing about most of the night."

"Well, if you two want to take your positions on the mattress," Madison nodded. "I'm sure I'm not the only one excited to watch a woman make love to another woman."

After Emma and I crawled onto the mattress, she sat behind my back, curling her legs gently around my hips. I could feel her cool breath on the nape of my neck, and as she brushed my hair to the side and began kissing me softly, I felt goose bumps rising on my skin. She technically hadn't yet revealed which body part of mine she wanted to focus on, and I smiled watching the rest of the group peering at us with a curious expression as Emma softly caressed the back of my neck.

But as she began kissing me slowly down the center of my spine, she pushed me further and further forward, until my shoulders were resting on the floor with my ass pointing up toward her face. As she began unzipping my jeans and pulling them down my legs, at first, I thought she intended to focus on my anus. But as she pulled my pants further down toward my knees while kissing my buttocks, I leaned further forward, tilting my dripping pussy up toward her face.

She paused for a moment, staring at my glistening snatch, then she rolled over onto her back, sliding her face under my splayed legs and resting her head in the cradle of my bunched-up jeans. While she peered up at me from between my legs, I smiled at her, running my fingers through her soft, corkscrew hair. As she turned her head to kiss the insides of my slippery thighs, I slowly lowered my steaming pussy onto her beautiful rosebud lips.

When I felt my vulva make contact with her mouth, I

gasped, remembering what it felt like to touch her for the first time in the privacy of our two-person tent up at the lake. Emma nibbled on my outer labia for a few minutes, pinching me teasingly between her front teeth, and I groaned watching her pretty face buried in my warm snatch. While she licked and nibbled me closer toward my burning clit, I tilted my hips forward, resting the crack of my ass over her chin.

I glanced around the circle, noticing the rest of the group stimulating themselves once again, then I peered back at Emma and smiled.

"Yes, baby," I purred, stroking her hair. "Kiss me the special way you do. Let's show these guys how to properly go down on a girl."

Emma nodded, then reached around the sides of my hips to pull my crotch harder down toward her face. I tried spreading my legs further apart, but the jeans bunching around my knees restricted my movement, so I sat further back, pressing my dripping cunt harder onto her face. When she felt my hard pubis pressing against her jaw, she retracted her lips while I rubbed my hardening clit against her teeth.

At first, I was happy to hump her face as my pleasure continued to build, but before long I wanted to feel her lips on my clit, and I raised myself up a few inches to let her peer at my erect gland. While I rolled my hips tantalizingly above her raised head, she tried to lick me with her tongue, but instead I held my snatch barely out of reach, dripping my juices onto her face.

She smiled back at me, rolling her tongue around the edges of her mouth, then she pulled my hips back down over her face, sucking my hard nub into her mouth. While she slathered my bean with her tongue, I clenched my fists in her hair, leaning further forward, pressing my weight harder down onto her. Since we'd done this before, she didn't panic, instead, threading her hands upward under my brassiere to squeeze my breasts as I began to rock my hips harder against her glistening face.

Somehow, she looked even prettier with my shiny lubrication coating her rosy cheeks, and as I moved ever closer to a climax, I smiled watching the rest of the group jerking and jilling themselves while they watched Emma eating my cunt.

"Shall we give them a little extra surprise for their viewing pleasure?" I whispered to Emma, humming happily as she lapped up my juices.

She nodded and I waited for just the right moment, then when I passed over the point of no return, I lifted my hips six inches above her head, gushing hard jets of fluid all over her blinking eyelashes. There was something incredibly erotic about cumming all over her pretty face, and while I grunted in delirious pleasure a few feet above her, she groaned in unison with me, enjoying my impromptu shower almost as much as I did.

8

W hen I returned to my place in the circle, I didn't even bother pulling up my pants, soaked as they were from my drenching orgasm. Instead, I placed my wet clothes on the floor beside me, crossing my legs while I peered back at the rest of the group with a bare midriff.

"Alright then," Madison said, adjusting herself distractedly at the foot of the mattress. "I'd say that gives a whole new meaning to the expression *wet kiss*. Why don't we all take another short break while I change the sheets? I think we've got time for one final round."

While she changed the bed linens, Lily and I chatted casually, awaiting the next pairing.

"It seems everyone's had a turn on mattress except *me*," she frowned. "My chances aren't looking good."

"I dunno," I said, watching Maddy collecting the cards. "It's funny how Madison seems to be picking us off one at a time. I think maybe she's holding a few cards up her sleeve."

After everybody resumed their positions, Madison paused as she peered around the circle.

"It's certainly been an interesting night," she smiled. "What do you guys think? Have you picked up a few extra kissing techniques this evening?"

"Damn right," Lily said. "I just wish I could experience it *first-hand* like the rest of the group."

"If you play your cards right," Madison said, reshuffling the deck in her lap. "You might still have a chance."

She tossed everyone a new card, and when Lily picked hers up, I peered over her shoulder, noticing she held an ace of hearts.

"Looks like you got your wish," I smiled.

"Yeah," she nodded. "Now I just have to decide whether I want to give or receive."

When everyone else showed their cards, this time it was Shae who had the lowest number.

"You said you wanted the roles *reversed* earlier," I said, watching Shae eyeing Lily up while she squirmed excitedly on the floor. "Here's your chance to give her girl cock a little extra oral love."

"Okay," Madison said, peering at everyone's card. "It looks like Lily holds the high card and Shae has the lowest. And because you have an ace, you get to choose whether to give or receive this time, Lily. Have you decided how you'd like to play this turn?"

"Um-hmm," Lily nodded, staring at Shae's crotch in her tight jeans. "But I'd like to keep it as a surprise until we come together on the mattress."

"Works for me," Maddy smiled, turning toward Shae. "How about you, Shae? Are you ready for a no-holds-barred final round?"

"I'd have it no other way," Shae winked. "With my special set of features, I'd rather Lily wait to view my buffet before taking her first bite."

When the two women crawled to the center of the circle, they kissed softly for a few moments, then Lily pressed Shae down onto the mattress, kneeling over her in a sixty-nine position while she began to unbutton Shae's pants. When she pulled them down over her hips and Shae's large cock sprung out, some of the participants gasped, not realizing the pretty girl was actually transgender.

While Lily dragged her jeans down over the bottom of her legs, Shae dry-humped her stomach, squeezing Lily's ass from behind. Lily placed her hands under Shae's knees and bent them up softly, then she leaned down to lick the tip of Shae's dripping dick with the end of her tongue. Shae groaned and lifted her hips off the mattress, and Lily lowered her head, tracing a line down the underside of Shae's instrument with her tongue.

When she planted her face between her thighs, we heard a strange slurping sound, and everybody peered at one another with a surprised expression. But it didn't take long for the enigma to be revealed, as Lily slowly pulled Shae's knees toward her, tilting her hips upward to reveal her glistening gash. Instead of the usual testicles nestled under her cock like most transgender she-males, Shae was a true hermaphrodite, with a fully functioning set of both male and female sex organs.

As Lily curled her hips further forward and lifted her ass higher off the mattress, Shae spread her legs wide apart, revealing her bouncing hard-on and her dripping vulva for the whole room to see. Everybody groaned at the incredible sight of the sexy ladyboy displaying her bifunctional sex organs, and it didn't take long for them to pull off the rest of their underclothes and begin stimulating themselves unabashedly while they watched Lily kissing and sucking Shae's perineum.

Although Lily was technically kissing more than one body part, Madison didn't seem to mind, pulling her own pants down to the bottom of her knees while trilling her pussy as she took in the erotic show with the rest of us. When Lily pulled Shae's upturned ass further toward her, she licked her tongue along the full length of her slit, teasing her until she reached her pink pucker. Without any hesitation, she rolled her tongue along the outside of the rim, flicking the tip into her crevasse while Shae moaned and rocked her hips in delirious pleasure.

I wasn't sure if Lily knew exactly what she'd gotten herself into when she started this match-up, but from the look of the huge wet spot in the crotch of her jeans, she was apparently just as turned on as the rest of us, jerking and trilling ourselves as we watched the two lovers curled up in an upright sixty-nine position.

While Lily continued to rim Shae's sphincter with the tip of her tongue, she reached under her hips with her right hand and grasped Shae's dripping cock in her fist, jerking her off while licking and teasing her slit. Shae grabbed Lily's ass perched above her head, and reached around, beginning to unbutton her jeans. Lily shimmied her hips to help her pull her pants down, then she lifted each of her knees to allow Shae to pull them all the way off her legs.

By now, everybody's lower body was fully exposed, including my own while we shamelessly rubbed and fingered ourselves in a fever pitch of excitement. The sight of the two women licking each other's pussies was impossible to resist, especially with Shae's big phallus dangling between her legs. Although they had both far exceeded the game rules by touching more than the one target area, nobody including Madison seemed to mind as we groaned and panted along with them in simultaneous pleasure.

While Lily squirmed over Shae's face, pumping her dick with her right hand, she continued to lick and tease her dripping vulva and flaring sphincter with her tongue. It didn't take long for both women to begin squealing and grunting in mounting pleasure, and as they approached their climax, I peered around the circle, noticing the rest of the group gaping their mouths open in escalating pleasure, teetering on the edge of their orgasms.

When Shae started to shake her legs and her big dick began to squirt thick ropes of cum down over her stomach, no one could hold back any longer as Lily and the rest of us began jerking and convulsing in mutual ecstasy. I noticed even Madison hunched over, jerking heavily as she peered ahead at the erotic sight of the two women kissing and sucking one another in unbridled passion.

Jesus, I thought after everyone finally came down from their highs, slumping forward in exhaustion. *How will Madison ever top this wild and exciting party?*

But something told me this wouldn't be the last of her sex parties, and my pussy twitched at the thought of what she might have in store for us next time...

R*eady for more erotic chills and thrills? Download the next exciting story in* Jade's Erotic Adventures, *Pledge Week:*

*There's more than one way to be initiated to the pleasures of
lesbian sex...*

ALSO BY VICTORIA RUSH

Wet your whistle a hundred different ways with Jade's Erotic Adventures. Browse the full collection of Victoria Rush steamy stories here:

Click to scan your favorites...

FOLLOW VICTORIA RUSH:

Want to keep informed of my latest erotic book releases? Sign up for my newsletter and receive a FREE bonus book:

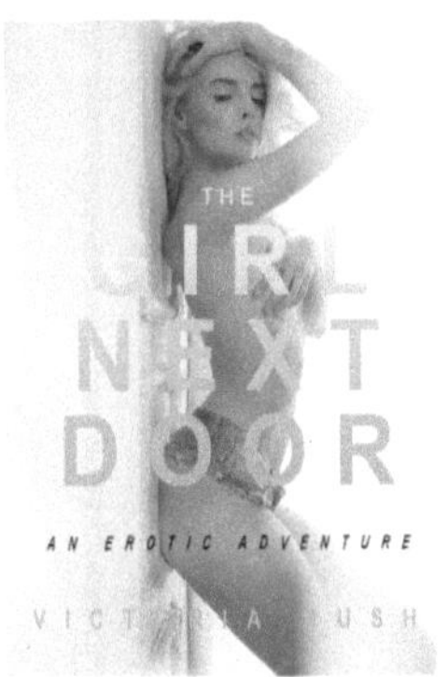

Spying on the neighbors just got a lot more interesting...